YOU ARE A LOVED GIRL

Inspiring Stories about Family, Friendship, Self-Confidence, and Love

Nadia Ross

Special Art Stories

YOU ARE A LOVED GIRL

Inspiring Stories about Family, Friendship, Self-Confidence, and Love

Nadia Ross

Paperback ISBN: 979-12-80592-80-4
support@specialartbooks.com
www.specialartbooks.com

This book is a work of fiction. Any resemblance to persons, living or dead, or places, events or locations is purely coincidental.

Table of Contents

Introduction

Hello, Amazing Girl!

Do you know that your parents, grandparents, and other family members love you very much? Did you know that your parents used to be the same age as you are now? They went through all the emotions and feelings you've experienced so far.

Loving you is the best thing they have ever gotten to do, and by reading this book with you, they will help you sort through similar thoughts and experiences. You and your family members can build an amazing bond together. This connection will create memories for you that will last throughout your lifetime.

You are a very lucky girl to have so many people love and support you. You can believe in yourself and bring your unique light into the world. Your relationship with your parents and family can give you confidence and help you spread your wings through the world.

Your relationship with your loved ones will inspire you to do things you may not have tried before.

This book contains many stories where unique characters go through a situation improved by their family's love. When you read this book, look to see if you can find similarities between your loved ones and you. Did you ever accidentally break something special? Have you ever played on a snow mountain? Did you ever dance with imaginary magical creatures in a forest? Have you ever helped your grandmother make something?

These characters do all of these amazing things, and they do it all with their families.

When you do things together, you will have incredible experiences, learn amazing things, and create a wonderful connection with your family. Find out how our characters connect with their families and see if there is anything you'd like to try with yours!

Talk to your family members, and ask them what they used to do when they were your age. Why don't you try asking them now? Mix your own creativity and magic into your questions and find out more about them today.

Come on, let's get inspired!

Snowday at Grandma & Grandpa's House

Everyone has a friend they love to be with. This friend might think exactly like you, laugh at the same things, and love everything you do. But, when you come across something new, and your friend helps you experience it, there may be some things you aren't prepared for. You may get scared, nervous, excited, or happy when this happens—you may feel all the feelings at once. But, if you experience something unpleasant, don't let that spoil your fun. Dust yourself off and try it again. You and your friend can have an amazing new thing together!

~ ~ ~

Marisa woke up to find frost covering her window. She rolled over and touched the window, which was very, very cold. It was so cold it was as if the ice from outside traveled down her finger. Instead of pulling away, she used the heat left in her hand to trace out the shape of a heart. The shape only stayed for a few moments after she pulled her finger away.

A gentle knock caused her to turn toward the door. She saw her mom coming into her room and rolled over. Marisa didn't usually mind going to school because she got to see friends and learn new things. But today she didn't want to get out of her warm bed.

Her mom sat on her bed and brushed the bangs out of Marisa's eyes, "Well, my dear daughter—you lucked out. School has been canceled because of the snow. You have a snow day."

Marisa's eyes widened. She had heard of snow days before but hadn't had one. "What does that mean?" She asked her mom.

"It means you and your cousin Dani get to spend the day with your Grandpa and Nona," her mom said.

Marisa leapt out of bed. "What?" she asked excitedly. "That's great!"

Her mom laughed and said, "Yep. It's time to get ready. We need to get your snow boots."

7

Before Marisa knew it, they were in the car headed over to her grandparents.

At the house, Marisa looked up, and saw her cousin Dani.

Dani, who was six months older, was also Marisa's best friend.

They ran up to each other, hugged, jumped around, and squealed "I can't believe we get to spend the whole day together!" Dani yelled.

Marisa shouted, "Yes! With NO SCHOOL!"

Dani whooped, "We get to play in the snow!!

Marisa stopped for a second. "I haven't ever played in the snow."

Dani bounced back and forth on her feet and said, "Then I will teach you!"

Nona approached the girls and put a hand on each of their shoulders. "Alright, girls, go ahead to the kitchen. I have some hot food for you to eat and something to drink before you go outside. The warm food will keep the chill away."

For breakfast, they had delicious baked cinnamon apples. Their Nona was good at cooking every-thing. Marisa heard her mom call goodbye but had her mouth full of food and couldn't call back so she waved out the window as her mom drove away.

Once the girls were done eating, Grandpa came in to help them clean up their dishes. He gave them a toothy smile and raised an eyebrow, "Are you girls ready to go outside?"

"Yes!" they both shouted.

~ ~ ~

With every *crunch, crunch, crunch* of the snow, Marisa struggled to stand. She hadn't expected walking in the snow to be so hard. They tried to play tag, but she kept falling over, and they both realized that tag was not fun if one person couldn't run. Then, they tried to build a snowgirl, but even though there was a lot of snow, it wasn't good at sticking together—their snowgirl just kept falling apart.

Feeling a little defeated, they saw their grandpa walk outside. He was sweeping the front porch off and called to them. He said, "Why are you girls just standing around?"

Dani tried to brush the scarf away from her mouth but had difficulty because of her mittens. Marisa laughed at how silly her cousin looked. But when Dani got it, she said, "We don't know what to do. We can't build a snowgirl because the snow isn't packing right, and Marisa can't run in the snow yet because it's too high. So, we're trying to figure out what to play next."

Their grandpa came down the stairs and walked down the driveway. He turned to the street and waved his arms at a big truck coming down the road. "Marty!" he called, "Hey! Hey! Marty! Come on over here!" Grandpa motioned for the plow to push the snow into his front yard.

Grandpa stomped back up the driveway away from where Marisa and Dani were standing. They watched as the snow plow pushed a big pile of snow forward with one motion. Then, it moved backward and pushed another big pile of snow onto the first.

When Marty, the snow plow driver, finished piling up a big bank of snow, both girls stood before the large pile in awe. "Woooooaaah," they said together. They both looked at each other, smiled and took off running toward the mountain of snow.

It didn't matter to Marisa that she fell over a few times. She was in awe of how much snow was in one

place and that falling into tufts of snow didn't hurt. All Marisa could do was just laugh.

Dani made it to the snow mountain first. When she got to the top, she sat down and slid on her back into her grandparent's front yard. Marisa thought it looked amazing. She decided that was the first thing she wanted to do. She climbed up the mountain to meet her cousin.

Marisa sat at the top of the pile, she looked around the neighborhood. Everything was white and crisp. Marisa fell in love with the snow. It was the best thing she'd ever seen.

After enjoying the sight of the snow, she pushed herself over the top and wooshed downward. She hit the ground with a *thaaawwwummmp*, and a huge puff of snow surrounded her. She rolled over in laughter.

Then, she sat up with an idea.

"Dani, let's build a snow fort—we can pretend we live in Alaska and we have penguins for neighbors."

"Yes!" Dani rocked back and forth with excitement, "We can burrow a little hole in the snow mountain and pretend they live there while we have another hole. You dig one, and I will dig one. Then, we can have a snowball fight with the penguins."

Marisa loved that idea.

After a few moments, she had a hole big enough for their imaginary penguin neighbors to play in. Then, she went around to help Dani build the spot for the both of them. They couldn't make the hole too deep, but it was big enough for both of them to fit in.

Dani and Marisa sat in it for a few minutes, as they tried to catch their breaths.

Marisa did what Dani asked, but she had trouble forming the balls since the snow was so soft. She turned around to let Dani know and was smacked in the face by something cold and hard.

Marisa was so surprised, she couldn't even speak. Instead, she plopped down to the ground. She held up her hand to her face and brushed away the snow.

The sting of the snowball on her cheek made Marisa start to cry. She could hear Dani yelling her name, but the pain throbbed along her cheek, and as she held her hand to her face, her mitten got wet with tears.

"Oh, no!" Marisa heard Dani call, "I'm so sorry! I didn't mean to hit you!" Marisa could hear Dani starting to cry too.

Then, through the tears, Marisa heard Nona call their names, "Are you girls okay?"

Dani yelled back, "No. I accidentally hit Marisa with a snowball, and she's hurt!"

Although Marisa knew that it was an accident, she couldn't help but be a little angry with her cousin. This anger rose a little more because she was having too much trouble getting out of the snow. She rocked back and forth, trying to figure out how to stand, and kicked her feet and arms. She couldn't move and started to cry harder.

The tears stopped quickly as Marisa felt two strong hands lift her and help her to her feet.

"Ah, come on, girls. We can go inside for a few minutes. If you both keep crying, the tears will freeze on your face, and you'll be no good to anyone."

Marisa couldn't help the slip of laughter.

When the girls got to the stairs, their tears grew, and they were more upset. Dani was getting worked up because Marisa was crying, and Marisa cried harder because Dani was crying.

Marisa tried to burble, "Dani hit me with a snowball!"

Dani wailed, "I didn't mean to! I don't want to hurt you!"

In their grandparent's living room, Nona and Grandpa helped them strip off their snow gear and wiped away their tears.

"Okay," Grandpa looked at Marisa's cheek, "It just looks a little red." He wiped away her tears as Nona wiped away the tears from Dani's face. "No harm done there."

Marisa sniffled, "I was just surprised."

"Ah." Nona said, hugging Dani, "If you're going to have a snowball fight, you must be prepared to be hit by snowballs."

Dani hiccuped, "We weren't trying to have a snowball fight with each other. I was trying to get the penguins!"

Grandpa cocked his head to the side, but then she saw a sparkle perk up in his eyes like he realized what was happening. "Ah. Those penguins were getting ready to start a fight with you, huh? But it's no big deal having a snowball fight with each other. That's what kids are supposed to do in the snow."

"I don't want to fight with Dani," Marisa said.

Nona looked at Marisa and she rubbed her cheek, "It's not a real fight, my sweet girl. It's a fun way to play in the snow."

Marisa looked over at Dani, who nodded and said, "I am so sorry that I hit you when you didn't know the rules.

Grandpa rubbed his whiskered chin and said, "Ah! That was the problem. There was a miscommunication! We have to teach Marisa the rules of snow!"

Marisa perked up. She got an idea, "Then play with us. You can teach me!"

So Grandpa, Nona, Dani, and Marisa went outside and started playing with their imaginary penguin friends. They all had a snowball fight together.

Although Marisa couldn't wait to get home to tell her parents about how much fun she had, she didn't want the day to end either.

They continued playing in the snow for a long time and only went in when they needed a break. It was the best first snow day ever!

~ ~ ~

Arguments can happen when you misunderstand others. Be sure to really listen and understand the other person's point of view. When we fight with someone we love, it doesn't mean they don't love us anymore, you simply have to work things out together. Having other people who care about you can help bring you back together.

Pot & Pan Rock Band

What do you do when you want to play a game, but others don't want to join in? Do you get frustrated or annoyed? Wouldn't it be good to try what the other person wants to try? You'll be surprised by what

happens when you approach a new idea with an open mind.

~ ~ ~

Natalie, her mom, and Mikey, her brother, sat around a coffee table playing a card game. Laughter broke loose throughout the living room. It was so loud that it echoed across the room.

Buzz. Buzz. Buzz. The phone on the table vibrated, and the cards in the center bounced.

"Uh-oh. It's a number from work." Natalie's mom looked at Natalie and rolled her eyes toward her daughter with a little smile. Then she picked up her phone, "Hello?"

Natalie rolled her eyes a little. She knew what was about to come but wasn't looking forward to it. Her mom worked from home, and while that meant she sometimes had to do things when they were all playing together or when the kids had a day off, it also meant that Natalie would have to watch her little brother Mikey for a little while too.

Natalie thought her brother was okay.

She looked over to see him hunched over on the floor looking at something underneath the refrigerator. He was still wearing his pajamas and not even in his daytime clothes yet. Natalie rolled her eyes.

He wasn't bad but he could be annoying most times.

She looked at him while listening to her mom in the background.

"Natalie?" She turned her attention to her mother, "I have to take this. Can you play with Mikey?" Natalie sighed again, but she knew it wouldn't help her mom, so she nodded quickly after it and pretended that the sigh didn't happen.

When Natalie turned her attention to her brother, he smiled at her. He had a goofy smile, showing all his teeth and big saucer eyes that made him so cute. Natalie couldn't help but smile. "What do you want to do," she asked her brother.

Mikey shrugged, "Count the nails in the walls?"

"We have to do something to keep busy while Mama is on the phone. She won't be long, but let's entertain ourselves," Natalie straighten herself up, lifted her chin, and did the best impression of her mom she could when she said, "We don't want to get in her hair."

"Okay," Mikey said. He pushed himself up to standing and blinked his brown eyes at her, "What should we do?"

Natalie stood too and looked around the house. "Um . . . do you want to play a game?"

She looked at her brother. He shrugged.

Then, she remembered why she was sometimes annoyed with him. Mikey could never make a decision.

And, when Natalie chose for him, he never wanted to do what she picked.

Natalie huffed. "Well, let's go look at the games then."

They walked down the hall together and looked up at the shelf of board games they had.

"Do you want to play checkers?"

"No," Mikey harumphed.

"Chess?"

"No."

"Do you want to build blocks?"

"No."

"Do you want to paint?"

"No."

"Do you want to read?"

"No."

"Do you want to pretend to be spies?"

"No."

"Do you want to build a fort?"

"No."

"Do you want to color?"

"No."

Natalie's patience got erased with every 'No' she heard from Mikey. She tried to take a deep breath and release it to keep herself calm, as her mom told her. She closed her eyes and pictured a happy place that would relax her.

When she closed her eyes, she saw the forest with a pink couch sitting between two pine trees. The sun was shining, and there was a waterfall in the background. She could almost hear the birds singing.

She let a long breath out and felt better. When she opened her eyes to see her brother, she said, "Let's play basketball!" It was a good idea. It was outside so that they would get fresh air, and her brother liked to pretend he could dunk the ball. Her excitement rose because she knew this was the right thing to do.

Natalie took his elbow and started to walk him toward the back door.

"No," Mikey said.

Natalie turned around to look at him. "What?" she asked.

"No. I don't want to play basketball."

The last bit of Natalie's patience got swiped away. It was gone.

"Fine," she said. "Find something to do yourself."

She let go of her brother's arm, spun on her foot, and marched back to her room.

Back in her bedroom, Natalie flopped down on her bed. She stared up at the ceiling and blew out a big breath. She was sad that she had lost her patience with her brother and wasn't doing what her mom asked her to do. She wished she could find a way to keep her patience and remember that Mikey wasn't doing it on purpose.

She closed her eyes again and thought about her happy place.

Her mom was sitting on the big pink couch with her this time. Her mom said the thing that she always said to make Natalie feel better, "Instead of getting frustrated, be open to other people's ideas. You never know where they can take you. Even if it sounds a little crazy."

Natalie opened her eyes again and smiled. Her mom didn't believe in making mistakes. She only believed in learning lessons.

Natalie took that message with her as she stood up and went back down the hall to find her brother.

As she was coming close to the kitchen, she heard loud noises.

Bang!

Bash!

Bang! Bang!

Bash!

Natalie hurried into the room and saw Mikey sitting on the floor. He had a pot and pan sitting in front of him. They were flipped upside down, and he was hitting the bottoms with a wooden spoon to make noise.

"Look, Natalie! I found something to do!" Mikey said with his goofy smile.

Natalie smiled back and said, "Yep, you did! Lemme get a spoon, and I can do that with you if you give me one of those?"

Mikey nodded. Natalie sat next to him, and they beat on the pots for a few moments.

"Hello, my musical children!"

Both Natalie and Mikey whipped their heads toward their mother's voice.

"I'm almost done, but I want to join your rock band when I get off the phone. Why don't you do a rock band outside?"

Natalie realized their pot and pan music was too loud for their mom's work call. She nodded and took Mikey outside.

They marched around banging on the pans and pots until their mom came out with them. Together all three made some pot and pan rock music in their pot and pan rock band.

Mikey used two spoons and a pot to hit the beat *rat-ta-tat-tat, ratta-tat-tat.*

Natalie scratched her pan with a wire brush that went *scrrrreeeeeeeaaaaaaaaaa, shuffle-shuffle.*

And Mom started to bang on their plastic containers with a *bop-ditty-bop-ditty-bop-bop.*

When they got into a good rhythm, Mikey started to sing "I'm making a rock band with my M'am and sis. We be on pots and pans, and one day will have a ton of fans!"

Natalie and Mikey didn't have much trouble finding things to do together after that day. And their mom had an amazing time playing in their rock band whenever she could.

~ ~ ~

The best experiences can sometimes happen spontaneously. You don't have to plan everything to be creative and have fun. Be open to other people's ideas; you never know what you might miss out on until you try. Participating in something new can open up a world of possibilities you might never have imagined otherwise.

The Trail to Treasure

What do you do when you miss someone so much because they have to go away? Sometimes the people who love and care for us have responsibilities and need to travel. Do you write them notes? Talk to them on the phone? Do you send them little gifts? How do you show them how much you miss them? Would you like it if they did something to let you know how much they love you?

The adventure below has an amazing treasure hunt showing the girls how much their dad loves them. Keep reading, and you'll find out how!

~ ~ ~

"Hey, girls: your dad is on a video call for you. Are you awake?"

Elisabeth rolled over and opened her eyes. When her mother's message sank in, she sat straight up as joy shot through her body. "June!" Elisabeth said, jumping out of bed. She ran over to shake her younger sister awake. "June. Get up! Dad is waiting to talk to us."

June opened one eye to grumble at Elisabeth for waking her up. June squinched her eye shut again and threw her arm over her head.

Elisabeth danced on her toes. She did not want to wait for June to wake up. Normally, she would gently lull her sister out of her sleepiness, but she was too excited to see her dad on video chat. She turned around and sat on her sister's bed. Elisabeth began bouncing. "June! Dad is waiting to talk to us! Wake up!"

June grumbled again, then said, "What?" She sat up, "Dad?" June's blonde hair was sticking out in places that made her look like someone had rubbed a balloon over her head. Elisabeth giggled, and June scowled, waiting for her sister to say something about her hair.

June pressed her hands to her head to try to get her unruly hair back into place, but she quickly gave up as soon as her mom turned their tablet around to show their father smiling back at them.

"Hi, girls!" He said and waved. He had a big smile spread over his face. His beard only made his features seem warmer. His brown hair was combed neatly to the side, and his blue eyes crinkled on the side as he saw his daughter's excitement.

"When are you coming home?" June asked excitedly.

"Soon, girls. But, since I'm not able to be home yet. Your mom and I set up a special treat around the house for you."

Elisabeth went to ask a question, and June interrupted her, scrambling closer to the edge of the bed to see her father. "What is it?"

Elisabeth laughed at her sister's excitement but didn't say anything.

Their dad laughed, saying, "Your mom made you a treasure hunt. You have to work together to find the special treasure. You'll have to find items around the treasure path, and they will lead you to the next clue. Your mom has a list of the items and made a map that will help you follow the trail."

"We miss you so much, Daddy!" Elisabeth said, her emotions ballooned up and were ready to spill over into tears. She didn't know just how much she missed having him around until she saw his face. She closed her eyes and tried to remember what his arms felt like while hugging her. But, she couldn't. She was happy to speak with him, but it was no comparison to having him home.

June agreed, "Yes! We want to see you now!"

Their dad nodded, "I feel the same way, girls. I'll be home in a few days and know that I miss and love you very much. I can't wait to see you too. The first thing I will do is scoop both of you up into a monster hug."

The girls opened their arms as wide as they could go. They stood on their tip toes and wrapped their arms around themselves. "ROAR!" All three of them shouted together. It was something they did when they were apart and when they were together.

The girls scrambled to get up. They ran to the door bouncing around. They tried to get past their Mom, "Remember what your dad said. This is a team effort. You have to work together to find the clues and be together when you start."

"Okay!" June said, "Come on, Elisabeth!"

The girls ran downstairs to find their Mom waiting for them. She handed each girl a list that had several items on it.

The letter said:

Hello, my lovely girls: Please find the rhyme down below. Each line will tell you just where you should go.

An egg that's green and sits in the cold.

A breakfast word that rhymes with roast.

Where our pup wipes his feet.

A purple leaf where our visitors meet.

Toys that you play with in sand and wind.

The flower that's yellow and that we wave to hello.

A smiling tree is where the treasure will be.

"Good luck, girls." Their Mom said with an amused smile. Elisabeth watched her Mom walk away, "You're not going to help us?"

Their Mom shook her head, "Nope.You won't find me until the end of the treasure hunt."

"What's to stop us from following you right now?" said June.

"Well, that wouldn't be half as fun, would it?" Their mom said, and she disappeared around the corner.

Even if June tried to make things easier, Elisabeth wanted to have fun and find the clues. She wouldn't let June take the easy way out.

"Okay!" Elisabeth said, "It looks like we have to get the green egg first."

June nodded and said, "I think it's in the basement."

Elisabeth shook her head, "We aren't going to the basement. There isn't a green egg down there. I bet it's in the refrigerator."

"Why would it be there? Any green food in the refrigerator gets thrown out by Mom." June said, "I've tried to eat some of it, and she wouldn't let me."

Elisabeth rolled her eyes again at her sister. "That's because the green food you tried to eat was rotten. Mom and Dad wouldn't let us look for rotten food."

June shrugged and said, "I still think the basement is a good place to start."

Elisabeth sighed. She knew how to shut down that idea, "Fine. Let's go look in the refrigerator, and if the green egg isn't there, we can check out the basement."

June smiled and said, "Yes!"

The girls walked into the kitchen, opened the refrigerator, and there was a very green, very big plastic egg. Elisabeth beamed, throwing June an 'I told you so' look. June huffed and crossed her arms.

Elisabeth reached into the refrigerator and pulled out the plastic egg. The egg was so large that she had to hold it with two hands. "Can you take the lid off, June?" June nodded, excited to be part of the first step. June took out the paper that would lead them to the next clue.

"Think about your favorite food. What always puts you in a good mood? Remember the clue that rhymes with roast, sugar, and spice in a nice dose."

June and Elisabeth thought about it for a few moments. June jumped up when she realized that the word spice meant cinnamon. "Elisabeth, it's cinnamon toast!"

"Yes!" Elisabeth agreed.

The girls quickly ran to the toaster. They found a piece of paper under the toaster that was in the shape of a piece of toasted bread with cinnamon. Elisabeth flipped it up and read, "When you see the dog paw, you'll be on the front lawn."

June turned to go out the back door. Elisabeth stopped her. "That's not the right way to go."

"But the door is right here," June stomped. "Why should we go to the front of the house?"

"Because the clue is talking about the 'pup rug.' That's at the front of the house" They always wiped off their dog's feet when he came from outside.

"We don't have to listen to the clues, Elisabeth," June said, starting to get mad that her sister was trying to lead the way. June knew she had good ideas, too, and wanted her sister to listen to her.

"Yes, we do. Our parents did this puzzle for us to do together. They want us to follow the rules so we can do it right."

June sighed. She knew that Elisabeth was right. She rolled her eyes and said, "Fine."

They raced outside and found the paw print welcome mat. Under it was the next clue. But they didn't have to go far since they were at the door. Elisabeth said, "this is where our visitors meet. Look for a purple leaf."

June turned around to see the wreath on the door, and it was circled with different color leaves. She saw a note sticking out from one that was purple. "Elisabeth! There's the leaf! Can you reach the note?"

This note said, "The sand and wind toys are not a mirage. It's time to go to the back of the house and the building called the garage."

"Let's go!" said June. She jumped up and realized how much fun it was to figure out the clues. She started to get excited that Elisabeth had made her follow them. But she wasn't going to admit it to her sister.

In the garage, the girls found their beach toys. The next clue said, "think about where we say hello. You'll find the garden and our flower that's yellow."

Elisabeth and June looked for the flower. It was easy to find because the girls bought their mom a Daffodil plant for her birthday last year. Everyone in their family always said 'Hello!' to the flower each time they saw it because it was bright and cheerful. They went over to see a note hanging off one of the stems.

It said, "Turn around and walk ten paces. You'll see a tree with some smiling faces."

The girls turned around and saw their favorite tree with a picnic lunch set up around it. Their mom had hung paper decorations and set up a table decorated with amazing-looking treats and fancy plates. When they ran over to the table, they started yelling,

"Wow!"

"This is incredible!"

And then, they stopped because they saw that their dad and mom had walked out from behind the garage. Their dad kneeled and opened his arms wide. The girls screamed and ran to him. They were instantly scooped up in a monster hug.

Elisabeth and June were crying happy tears as they looked at their mom and said, "Thank you for the wonderful surprise! The scavenger hunt was great!"

Their dad put them down, and they hugged their mom fiercely. She said, "I'm so glad you worked together and found your way to this amazing party."

"We are too!" They shouted. They took their dad's hand and walked over to the table. And all four faces were smiling under the tree as they ate sweet treats and listened to their dad's stories about traveling.

They were back together, and a warm sense of love and comfort settled over the family as they enjoyed the rest of their day.

~ ~ ~

Your family loves you so much. They will go to incredible lengths to show you how much they care and how special you are to them. Even though your loved ones sometimes have to be away from you, they miss you and still want to give you the best life they can. When you work together, you can enjoy what your family does for you even more.

Off to College (with Mom) We Go!

Sometimes we have to remember that our parents are more than just parents. They have jobs, friends, and things they love to do outside of being a mom and dad. Your parents sometimes even want to learn more at school! When your parents go to college, even grownups, they search for something better for

them and you! Find out what happens when Sabrina goes to college with her mom. Do you think that she will like it?

~ ~ ~

"Hey, Sabrina—I've got some bad news for you." Sabrina's mom sat down and looked at her with a big frown on her face.

Sabrina put her book down and sat up to look at her mom.

"Chelsea got sick," her mom explained. "She can't watch you today. You'll have to come to school with me tonight."

"What?" Sabrina asked, completely shocked.

"I have an exam I have to take. I'll be gone for longer than normal. You'll have to come with me, but be quiet because other people are taking a test too."

Sabrina rolled her eyes but stood up anyway. "I want to stay by myself." She crossed her arms over her chest. She was nine years old, after all. It was a good age to be alone.

Sabrina stomped her foot down and squinched her face. "I am not a baby. I can take care of myself." She often felt like her mom always had something to do and they didn't have time to spend together. Anger poked inside her chest.

Her mom knelt and placed her hand on her shoulder. Although Sabrina was annoyed, looking into her mom's eyes let calmness wash over her just a little.

"You know I can't let you do that. I don't want to leave you tonight. I know that it isn't something you want to do. I will not be in school forever; this is my last big test. You've been such a huge part of my going to school, and I appreciate how you've cared for and loved me through it. After this test, I'll find one job and won't have to work so hard between school and work. Okay?"

The last of the annoyance Sabrina felt with her mom melted away. She reached out to hug her. Her mom was always good at helping Sabrina feel better.

She wasn't happy about going to college for the night, but she would do it for her mom. As Sabrina walked down the hall to her room and tried to picture what college was like, she wondered if it was just like her school, but only bigger.

A lot of questions about college started to pop up in her mind. She realized that while her mom had been in college for the last few years, she knew very little about it. She wondered if there would be a lot of other grownups running around. Would there be any other kids her age walking with their parents? What were the teachers like? Did they have a school cafeteria? Did her mom have recess? Was there a giant playground where all the adults played? Were the teachers super old?

On and on, questions came into her head.

Once they were in the car and driving to college, Sabrina started asking her mom questions.

"What is your classroom like?"

"It's a large room with desks and chairs in it. It kind of looks like your classroom."

"But bigger," Sabrina asked.

"Just a little bit. It's got windows and a checkered floor, and the teacher's desk is in the front of the classroom. Just in front of the board."

"What kind of board is it?" Sabrina asked. Her school had just put in digital computer screens instead of the whiteboards they used to have.

"Chalkboards."

"What is a chalkboard?" Sabrina tried to imagine a board made of the colorful chalk she used to draw on her driveway, but thought that would be hard to use.

"It's a long green board on the wall where the teacher, or anyone with permission, can write on, but they use chalk."

"Oh." That sounded more fun to Sabrina, "How do I get permission to write on the board?" She really enjoyed playing with chalk and often made pictures on Saturdays on their driveway when it wasn't raining.

Her mom chuckled, "students only get to write on the board if the teacher needs them to answer a question. You probably won't be able to write on the board unless you ask the professor. But, I would like you to wait until everyone has turned in their exam if we are there that long."

Sabrina thought about her mom's request and decided it was good. She had to be respectful of the other students. "Okay, I will wait."

Sabrina didn't stop asking questions until her mom got into a big building with a lot of cars parked in it.

"What is that?" She asked her mom.

"It's called a parking garage. It's where all students of this campus put their cars, so they know it is safe and taken care of while we are in class."

They pulled into the garage and drove up a long ramp that circled around and up. Sabrina thought it was fun; each time her mom spun around a circle, they would go up another level, and Sabrina got to see many different cars.

When her mom parked, Sabrina's eyes grew wide as she got out and looked around. She had never seen so many cars.

"You look surprised," her mom said with a soft smile.

"I am! There are so many cars here. Do all the cars belong to other college students?"

"Mostly. Other adults and students work on campus too. So, some of those cars belong to those people. But there are more students than there are staff."

Sabrina nodded, impressed that so many people were going to school at night.

As she walked past the cars, she thought about what people wore—was everyone in their pajamas? Would they walk around carrying pillows? What was the difference between night school and day school? She bounced around her mom, waiting to find out.

She wanted to count how many cars she passed so she could see if she could estimate how many people were on campus, but instead, her mom led her over to a set of elevator doors.

Sabrina looked at her mom and blinked, "You get to ride in an elevator every day?"

"Yup."

"Can I push the buttons?"

"Of course,"

Sabrina pushed the button with the down arrow. It looked like V and turned green when she pressed it. It was great!

When the doors opened, she and her mom had to step aside to let some people out. When the elevator was empty, they walked in. "You can push the button now that says, 'G.' It stands for ground."

Sabrina did. The elevator jerked into motion, and they moved down. They stopped a few other floors, and more people got in and continued down to the ground level.

After the elevator ride, Sabrina and her mom started walking through campus.

The grounds were pretty. The buildings were very tall, and there were a lot of them. And between the buildings, weaved paved paths on which the students were walking, lined with grass, trees, plants, and statues.

Sabrina had an idea, "Mom! Can we look around? Everything looks so cool!" She craned her neck and saw something she thought was a play ground. She

looked around for other children her age. Instead, she stopped at a large building with a sign that said Library. "Woah," she whispered. It was much larger than the library she went to. She tried to imagine all the books she could read that were in there—she wondered if they had pictures.

"It's going to be dark soon, and I still have to take my exam."

Sabrina frowned a little and said, "Oh, yeah."

Her mom patted her hand, "Don't worry. We can come back here on the weekend and we can look around."

That perked Sabrina right up. She imagined coming here on a weekend when the weather was nice to look at all the statues and spend some time with her mom. It was a nice thought.

However, they continued walking to a building made of red brick and had tall black windows with extra corners that made it look as though the building had decks high in the sky. "Woah." Sabrina muttered under her breath—"You go to class here?"

"Yep. Some of my classes are in other buildings, but this is where my main classes are."

"What are you learning?"

"I am learning about the brain. It's called neurology. Sometimes people's brains don't work right and it makes them sick. I'm going to be a doctor to help people's brains get better."

Sabrina was shocked. She never knew her mom wanted to be a doctor. It sounded really neat and interesting. It was nice that her mom wanted to help people whose brains were sick. "It's no wonder why you go to school so much."

"Yes. Being a doctor takes a lot of school. But anything anyone does can only get better with time and experience."

Sabrina nodded and walked into the incredible building with her mom.

There was so much to look at.

There were people in a large sitting area to Sabrina's left.

There were offices, steps, and elevators to Sabrina's right.

People walked with their heads down, looking at their phones. Sabrina watched everyone mill through and around and in and out of one another. No one bumped into each other. It was like a dance.

"I can't believe this many people are out at night."

"Yes, it happens. Lots of people have to do many things to make their dreams happen. When they try

to achieve them, sometimes they have to find different ways to get there."

Sabrina thought that was a smart thing for her mom to say.

She connected the dots of her mom's life and thought that her mom was finding a way to make her dreams come true also.

Now she was really excited to see her mom's classroom.

The classroom was enormous. It didn't smell like a classroom she'd ever been in. Instead, it smelled very clean, like right after her mom cleaned the bathroom. There were long tables that seemed to run the entire length of the room. Long lights light up the room to make the room very bright.

Sabrina and her mom walked down a few steps to one of the tables closest to the teacher's desk. She sat next to her mom and started taking out her things.

"You'll have to be very quiet now, okay? Everyone will take their test, and no one can be disturbed. You're a very good girl. I know it will be hard to be quiet for so long."

She nodded to her mom. "I will do my best."

Sabrina swallowed when she thought about it. She hoped she could do it. She didn't know how long it would take.

She looked around the rest of the class. Many people had filed in and sat down to take their exams. She saw people tapping their pencils on their desks, one girl was twisting her hair around her fingers, and another guy had his head in his hands. He was muttering to himself a little. Sabrina smiled at that. She knew what it felt like to be nervous.

Sabrina took out her book and started to read while the minutes passed. When she got bored with her book, she wrote in her journal and finished making her bracelet. She didn't even notice how quickly the time passed, and soon, her mom stood up.

Sabrina watched her mom turn in her test and saw her smile with relief. Her mom looked at her daughter and made a funny face.

When her mom returned, they collected their stuff quickly and quietly to avoid disturbing anyone else and walked out of the room.

"You did so well, Sabrina. I think we should celebrate with some ice cream."

"You did well too, Mom! You should get sprinkles and an extra scoop of ice cream to celebrate your big exam."

Sabrina's mom laughed. "That is an amazing idea. Let's do that."

~ ~ ~

Your mom is more than just your mom. She takes care of you, feeds you, picks up after you, and so much more. But she is a person too! If you ask her questions, you'll find out how much of a smart, talented, and wonderful person she really is.

The Family Mural

Do you have anything that your family treasures above all else? Some families have antiques that are given to them from past generations. Other families make something special together. But, if your family has a keepsake that is so special that everyone enjoys it, what happens if something happens to it? If an accident occurs, and the piece your family loves so much gets broken, destroyed, or ruined, would you think of doing something new? Could you? If you use

your imagination and thoughts, bringing family love together can help you keep the specialness alive, even if there is a mishap.

~ ~ ~

On top of the mantel on a wall in a living room of a family just like yours sat a family photo of three sisters, their parents, and their grandparents. These nine people were very special to one another and the family photo meant so much to the family.

The rain beat upon the windows. It was coming down very hard and sounded a bit like drumming in a band. When Meredith inhaled she could smell the dewiness of springtime.

Meredith sat on the living room couch, looking at the image of her family. The picture was of when she and her sisters were smaller. So when she saw it, she was reminded of her family. Three of her grandparents in the photo were no longer around and, while she did miss them, she had a hard time remembering them because it had been a long time.

"Jen! Don't do that!" Jessica shrieked.

"Jessica, stop!" Jen yelled back. "You just pulled my hair!"

"Ow! I didn't mean to! Don't pull my hair back!"

"You just stepped on my foot!"

Every so often, she would look up to her sisters, who were twins and were wrestling around, and roll her eyes. She'd already told them a few times to settle down, but they refused to listen.

The girls couldn't go outside to burn their energy and instead of finding something quiet, they chose to do something loud.

Usually, Meredith didn't mind their rowdiness, but because they were stuck indoors, the twins found her no matter where she went.

Since there were five people in the house, the twins shared a room, and Meredith had her own, but their bathroom connected their room, and no matter how much Meredith tried to keep her door closed to find private time, today, the twins wouldn't have it.

Finally, Meredith decided to put her headphones on, listen to music, and read things on her phone. That was the best way she could get privacy, even if she was still in the living room with her sisters.

Jessica and Jen didn't seem to mind that Meredith was trying to ignore them, just as long as they were near one another.

Meredith shrugged her shoulders. If the twins broke something, it wasn't her fault. She wasn't in charge of watching her nine-year-old siblings; she was annoyed by them sometimes.

Meredith smiled at the joke to herself and swiped her finger up to read the next article.

CRASH!

Meredith's head shot up, and she ripped her earbuds out of her ears, "What happened?" she cried out. "Is anyone hurt?" She looked her sister's over and saw that while they were crying and shaking, they were not hurt. But Jen was pointing to a mess on the floor.

"Oh no!" Meredith moaned, "That's our family photo!"

She leaned over to pick it up and saw that, while the photo wasn't harmed, just a little wrinkled, the frame it was in was broken—it was a frame that had been in the family for a long time, and she didn't know if it was an heirloom or not. But she always remembered that the frame had been special to her mom.

With the crash, their parents came into the room, "Uh-oh. What is this?" Meredith's mom put her hands on her hips.

The twins started to cry even harder, their chins quivered, and large tears ran down their faces.

"We're sorry!" cried Jessica. Jen sobbed into her hands.

Meredith's dad came over and lifted the picture from her hands. He took Meredith by the elbow and led her out of the room. He rubbed his neck and said, "Can you take the girls into the basement? Mom and I will clean up the mess."

Meredith nodded to her dad and ushered her crying sisters out of the room. "We didn't mean to, please! We're so sorry!"

"It's okay. No one is mad. We just don't want you to cut yourself on the glass," their dad said.

Meredith led her sisters downstairs. While not as nice as the living room, the basement had some comfy furniture and a few games to keep the girls entertained. However, their excitement and energy had deflated with the broken picture frame.

Meredith tried to help her sisters feel better. "Do you guys want to play a game?"

"No," Jen said as she sank to the floor. She put her chin into her hand and looked up at Jessica, "Do you think mom and dad are mad we broke the family photo?"

Jessica kicked at the carpet and said, "Probably." She sat on a bean bag and laid her head back to stare at the ceiling. "We should have thought about the things we might break." She said as she slapped her hand to her forehead. "Why didn't we?"

Meredith suddenly felt bad, her sisters were sad, and would they have listened if she would have told them that they might break something? She bit her lip at the thought. While she didn't think they would have, she realized she still should have said something, even if she wasn't in charge of them.

"Hey, guys—don't feel bad, okay? Why don't we try to make it up to Mom and Dad?"

Jessica lifted her head from the bean bag chair, and Jen rolled her eyes up to look at Meredith. "How?" they asked together.

Meredith started to pace, she didn't have an idea yet, but if she thought for a moment, she knew something would come up. Some of the grandparents were no longer with them, so they wouldn't be able to rec-reate the actual photo again, but that didn't mean they couldn't recreate the image.

"Oh!" She said, "Why don't we make a mural?"

"What is a mural?" asked Jen.

"It is a bigger picture than normal and usually has a message."

"Why would we need to have a message?" asked Jessica.

"But we could sneak the picture from Mom and Dad and paint a mural of our family! Then, we could make it up to them. You know how much they love the pic-ture! And you know we can't have everyone pose for a new picture now."

Before she could say anything else, the twins ran up-stairs to talk to their parents, who were still clean-ing up the glass and mess. Meredith followed and squirmed when she heard.

"Not now. We can't take another photo like this. We have to clean up. Go. Get out of the room and find something to do."

The girls nodded slowly. Three of their grandparents were gone, and their grandma did live with them.

The twins padded out of the room and ran right into Meredith. Their faces fell. "Mom and Dad said no." Jessica's lip quivered again. She walked to the base-ment with her shoulders sagging.

Meredith stopped her and whispered, "They didn't say no. They didn't understand what you were asking because they were busy and didn't want you to get hurt."

"Maybe grandma would want to help?" Jen said.

Jessica perked up and said, "That is a great idea! Let's go ask her."

So the girls tiptoed up the stairs and found their grandma sitting at the kitchen table looking at the family photo. Their grandmother smiled when she saw her granddaughters, "Hello, girls. What can I do for you?"

The girls sat down, explained their issue, and then presented their idea, "Can you help us, please?" Jessica asked.

Their grandma nodded and said, "Of course! That would be lovely. Let's get some supplies and start the painting right away."

So they did.

Grandma drove them to the craft store, and they bought paint, brushes, and a big board on which they could paint. When they got home, Jen and Meredith started drawing out the images of their family members—they enjoyed drawing and painting a lot. They both wanted to be artists when they grew up. Jessica and grandma organized the paints and got everything ready.

When everything was set up, the rain had stopped, and the girls and their grandma decided that painting outside would be a great idea.

Jessica and Jen set up the mural board, and they all grabbed a brush and paint colors. Then, they started painting. They hummed to music and danced around.

Meredith accidentally painted their grandma's cheek, and they all burst out laughing. Their parents said, "What is going on here, now?"

Jessica smiled and said, "We're painting a family mural!"

"Oh! What a wonderful idea!" Her mom said, holding her hand to her heart.

"Do you want to help?" Meredith asked. She knew that if they all painted together, the activity and mural would be even more special.

"What a nice idea," said their dad. "Let's get some paintbrushes!"

The family spent the rest of the day painting a new family photo and had an amazing time doing it.

~ ~ ~

When we make mistakes, or things get broken, it's okay to feel sad about it. But, don't feel sad about it for long because it is an opportunity to create something incredible. You can use your imagination and grow closer together with your family at the same time.

Into the Forest!

What do you do when you are bored? Do you sit around and wait for someone to do something with you, or do you use that opportunity to be creative and try something you've never done before? When you find that you've nothing to do, but want to do something, use your imagination and find out where it can take you!

~ ~ ~

Charlie sighed.

Then, he sighed again.

Bryce scratched her head and raised her eyebrow at her brother, "Yes?" She asked. She was busy doing a puzzle but had difficulty finding the piece she wanted. She was beginning to grow irritated with the puzzle and her brother's noises.

Charlie rolled over on the footstool, which put his head upside down to look at Bryce.

"I'm bored," he said.

Bryce sighed. "Yeah. Me too." She said, dropping the puzzle piece she'd just picked up. "Let's go see what Mom and Dad are doing."

Charlie and Bryce followed the vacuum sound and walked into the living room. There they saw their parents cleaning. Their dad turned around and waved. He turned the vacuum off and said, "Hey, guys. What's up?"

Charlie ran to his mom's side and hugged her waist. She almost fell over from his weight but straightened out quickly. "We're bored," Charlie said.

Their mom patted Charlie on the shoulder and said, "That's fine. Boredom is just a reason to get creative."

"What?" Charlie said. He looked to his sister who shook her head and shrugged her shoulders. The idea that boredom could be a good thing sounded nuts.

"Will you play with us?" Bryce said in response.

"No," her dad said, "We have a bunch of cleaning to get done today. If you guys want to help us, you can. Otherwise, you'll have to find something else to do today. And try to do it together."

Bryce scrunched her nose at the idea—she had already done her normal daily chores and wasn't interested in doing extra stuff. She took out the garbage, cleaned her room, and cleaned out her parakeet's cage. She had enough cleaning. She looked over at Charlie and said, "Let's go see what we can find to do."

Bryce began thinking about what her mom said about getting a chance to be creative, and that gave her an idea.

"Come on, and I think we can have some fun." Bryce took Charlie's hand and led him outside. "Let's go into the woods. We can pretend we're on an adventure!"

"Okay! I want to search for buried treasure!" Charlie said.

The two walked into the forest behind their house, making a plan together as they went.

When Charlie and Bryce stepped into the woods, they looked around.

Everything was emerald green. It was sparkling with fairies and a unicorn ran by as a gnome chased a butterfly.

Instead of just trees and grass in their backyard, they saw tall trees with smiles on their trunks.

One tree waved them over with its branch and said, "Hello! Are you here to find the hidden treasure of your backyard?"

"Yes!" Charlie shouted.

Bryce nodded in agreement.

Bryce and Charlie thanked the tree and went on their way.

They climbed over hills and saw a wall of water in front of them. They realized the water was a waterfall made

of rainbows. Charlie and Bryce looked at each other. They knew if they walked through it, they would be all wet. But when Bryce looked over her shoulder, she saw no other way to go.

"Looks like we'll have to go through," Bryce said, blowing a big breath. Charlie nodded. He took her hand and held his nose—he didn't want to get any water up it.

When they came through the waterfall, they were dry!

They saw a pond with fish swimming. They looked like rubies, emeralds, and diamonds.

Charlie and Bryce could hear a sweet sound, and they looked around to see where it was coming from.

"The fish in this pond sing." They heard a voice say.

Charlie and Byrce looked around until they saw a chipmunk sitting in front of them. He wagged his tail and said, "I'm Chuck. It's nice to meet you. My friend the tree told me to take you down the path for a bit. We need to feed the bluebirds who will help you find the way to the treasure."

"What happens if you don't feed the birds?" Asked Bryce.

Chuck shuttered and said, "Ehhhhh, you don't want to know."

"Do you know what the treasure is?" Charlie asked the make-believe chipmunk.

Chuck swished his whiskers back and forth. He flicked his ears and looked around. He climbed onto Bryce's shoe and motioned for them to come closer to him so they could hear a secret.

When they leaned over, the chipmunk said, "No. I don't. Do you?"

Bryce and Charlie laughed and shook their heads. They didn't know what the buried treasure could be, but they were excited to find out.

Chuck led the kids down a path for a little way. Then, they saw one bluebird sitting on a tree. The bluebird whistled his song. And then, another bluebird appeared. They sang together, and two more bluebirds appeared. Soon there was a wall of bluebirds!

Chuck, the chipmunk, whistled to Charlie and Byrce. "You have to feed them special bird seed to get by."

They looked at each other and shrugged. Bryce looked around and said, "Ooh! Look!" She took a handful of small yellow-ish seeds from underneath a flower and said, "These could work!"

Charlie took some from her hand, and he threw them at the pretend wall of birds. He used his imagination to see each of the seeds landing in each one of the bird's mouths. Then, one by one, those birds blinked away.

After their encounter with the birds, Chuck said, "That was great! I'm happy to help. Come on let's go to the treasure!"

Chuck, Bryce, and Charlie found the mouth of a cave and decided to explore there. Inside the cave, they saw the golden light they thought the tree was talking about.

Chuck's tail twitched and he said, "Follow me!" Bryce crawled on her hands and knees. She turned back to see if Charlie was following her. Charlie nodded to his sister to keep going.

Bryce followed Chuck until he stopped. They had come to a place where they could stand up straight again. "Come on, Charlie! This way!" She shouted, pointed her finger into the air, and turned on her heel. She went racing to her right.

While they ran through the field, Charlie ran past his sister, and soon they were back in the trees. They saw a big golden X.

They jumped up and down and danced around, singing, "We found the treasure! We found the treasure!" They stopped and looked around. Chuck wasn't with them. Charlie and Bryce looked at one another.

"Where did he go?" Bryce asked her brother. Then, they looked over their shoulder because they heard a *SNAP!* "Bryce," Charlie said, "do you think that could be pirates?"

"Yes! Grab the treasure and let's run," she whispered.

They ran up to a tree, stuck their hand into a nook that had grown in its trunk, and pretended to pull something out. Charlie jumped up and down. He looked over his shoulder and said, "Oh no! They are after us!" He ran behind a tree.

Three big pirates with peg legs and parrots stalked in front of them. One of the pirates had an eyepatch over his left eye. Another only had two crooked teeth. The third one wore a blue bandanna around his head. But, Behind them, very small, Bryce could see Chuck creeping behind the pirates.

Charlie went to say something, but Bryce put her hand over his mouth. "Shhhhhh..." she whispered.

She was ready to call it quits when a strong arm grabbed her around her waist and pulled her back. Bryce squealed and kicked her legs, calling, "Charlie!" to get her brother's attention. He stopped and turned around to come to help her.

When Bryce was released, she turned around to see that her dad had come out to get them. She let out a sigh of relief and said, "Daaaa-ddd! You scared me!"

Her dad laughed and said, "Did you think I was a real pirate?"

Bryce laughed with her dad, "I didn't know what to think. We've been playing pretend for a while now. We got pretty creative with it. We talked to a chipmunk named Chuck, walked through a waterfall, explored a cave, fed a wall of bluebirds, and found a treasure buried in a tree. We've had a great adventure."

Charlie caught up to Bryce and her dad. He threw himself around his dad's legs making their dad topple over. Bryce fell over onto their dad too. Their imagi-

nary world fell away, and they were taken back into the backyard.

Bryce looked up and saw her mom standing over them with a big smile, "It looks like you guys found something fun to do!"

"We did!" Charlie said as he leapt up to his feet. "We used our imaginations, explored the forest, and met a chipmunk named Chuck." Bryce sighed, she knew she would miss Chuck. He was a good part of her imagination that she wished was real.

"That's great!" Their mom said, "Let's get some grilled cheese for lunch, and you can tell us about your adventure."

And their grilled cheese sandwiches never tasted so good.

~ ~ ~

Getting outdoors and connecting with nature is an incredible way to connect with someone you love. When you play make-believe, you use your creative mind in ways you might not have thought of otherwise. Use your imagination as often as you can. Bring your unique ideas together and have an amazing adventure!

When the Wood Whittles

Do you have a special person in your life that you look up to? Do they do something incredible you long to do? When the person you are closest to brings you into their hobbies, life, and their special universe, you'll learn something new while having an incredible experience with them. Each time you spend

moments together working on projects you love, you will grow closer and build an amazing bond.

~ ~ ~

Sara loved to visit her grandpa.

A warm feeling filled her heart each time she went to his house. Her grandpa's place always smelled like wood shavings and metal — he was a woodworker.

Sara couldn't go inside her grandfather's woodworking shop because there were a lot of tools that required adult supervision so that no one got hurt. She had gone in the room once with her dad and saw a lot of stuff with sharp edges that sparked in the light. She also heard many loud noises from the tools her grandpa plugged in.

She did not want to go in alone. But she would spend lots of time playing with the wooden toys he made and walking around his house looking at the statues, furniture, and other pieces he made.

Each one was like a piece of art. Her favorite piece was shaped like a horse. Its skin was crafted with a scraping tool that made ripples in the wood. When she ran her finger over the ripples, they were smooth and fit her fingertips perfectly.

So, when Sara visited her grandpa on a Saturday, she was excited to see the new things he had created. But, she didn't know he had a surprise waiting for her.

"Hi, Sara," Grandpa said. He leaned over and scooped her up into a big hug.

"Hi, Grandpa!" She responded, hugging him back.

"Guess what?"

"What?"

"We can go into the woodshop together today. You're old enough now and understand how to be safe."

"Oh." Sara was surprised but also nervous. Although her interest perked up, she had heard the loud machines and had been told how much she shouldn't go into the room for so many years; she hadn't been expecting the news.

"You're not excited?"

"No. I am, but it's a big room. What if I get lost? What if I accidentally do something I'm not supposed to and get hurt? What if I accidentally hurt you?" Sara could feel her panic rising with each question and didn't want to worry her grandpa. She knew it was a big responsibility and wanted to ensure she was ready for it.

Grandpa set her down and rubbed her back. "Don't worry. We are going to start with something small. We aren't using any of the big machines today."

Relief settled over Sara like a comfortable blanket.

"That's good," she sighed. "Those machines sound a bit scary."

Grandpa chuckled, "They can be if you're not used to them. But, I've seen how excited you get when you see new wooden creations, and I think you would like to make something too."

Sara nodded. She wanted to make something, but doubt wriggled in her mind, "But I don't know how to do something like that." She frowned a little and couldn't imagine making anything as amazing as her grandpa.

Grandpa took Sara's hand and led her through the house, "You won't know how to do something until you learn." He held his other hand up, "You don't have to do it if you don't want to, but you can't expect to know how to do something right off the bat. Knowing things comes with experience and time."

Sara thought about what Grandpa said. She thought it was smart, and she responded, "I do want to learn."

Sara bit her lip, it was the truth, even her hands shook a little at the thought.

When they reached the doorway of Grandpa's wood-shop, Sara let go of his hand. "I think I'm going to need a minute before I come in," Sara said. Her nerves about entering the room were bouncing in her belly like jumping beans, and she felt she needed to ramp herself up before stepping through.

"Would you like me to wait with you?"

Sara shook her head no.

She hadn't known how excited she was to make something until that moment.

As she stepped into the wood shop, her excitement turned to anxiety quickly. Everything was large and a little dark. There were big windows in the room on her left, but between her height and the way the shadows fell, it felt darker than what it might have been if she was taller.

"Grandpa?" Sara called meekly. He peeked out of a corner.

"I'm in the back of the room."

As walked toward her grandpa, curiosity took the place of her anxiety. She looked up and saw a big, long tool with a cylinder attached. She resisted the urge to touch it because she didn't want to break the rules or get hurt, but she wanted to see what the tool did. She hoped that she would be able to find out soon.

To her left, she saw other individual tools. They were all different shapes and sizes. They looked like forks, spooks, and knives, but these were thicker and thinner than the utensils she used to eat food with.

She took more steps and saw more tools.

Sara was so interested that She didn't even realize she'd come to the end of the pathway, and Grandpa was standing in front of her until he said, "Hello! You made it to my special place."

Sara started, then smiled, "You scared me a little bit."

"I saw that you seemed very interested in the tools. That's good! We'll get to those on another day. Today, I want you to sit down, take this gizmo and this block of wood and sit down next to me."

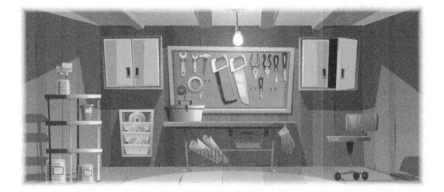

Sara looked around at the little nook Grandpa was sitting in. She loved it.

Windows surrounded the entire area. Four comfortable-looking chairs circled a small table in the middle, and buckets were next to each chair. When Sara looked inside the bucket on the side of her seat, she saw wood shavings inside of them. She looked up to Grandpa and gave him a big smile, "Are these buckets to keep the extra wood in?"

"Yep, my smart girl. It's hard not to make a mess when carving, but these buckets help."

Grandpa sat beside her and said, "But, I don't want you to worry about that now. I want you to focus on your first statue. See, I started it for you. But most beginners use a potato."

Sara took the statue her grandpa had started for her. "A potato?"

"Yep. It's the best way to learn from the beginning. That way, you get a feel for carving without worrying about safety."

Sara examined the potato—it was the head and arms of a squirrel. Although the details, like its eyes and fur, weren't carved in yet, she could see that Grandpa had also begun adding an acorn into it.

She looked between the vegetables and wanted to see how the squirrel would turn out, so she said, "I'll do the squirrel since it's already started. Just to see."

"Good choice." Grandpa said, "So, now let's get some gloves on you."

Sara nodded. She pulled on the gloves and was happy to see that they fit.

"The first lesson you should learn is to keep your tools sharpened. When you use dull tools, you can hurt yourself."

Sara made a mental note.

"This tool is called a gouge, and there are two ways to hold it," Grandpa explained. He showed her how to hold them by placing the handle in her palm. "Turn the blade up, it will give you the forehand grip. And the blade down will give you your backhand grip."

"Then, we will be using a method called a "push method."" Grandpa showed her how to push the gouge away from herself.

"There. You're doing great!" Grandpa said, rubbing his hands together, "Now, with more practice on the potatoes, we can move on to the wood."

Sara spent the rest of the day with Grandpa practicing carving potatoes and holding the gouge differently. She was very happy she didn't let her anxiety get in the way of carving her squirrel. She knew she took a big step today, and if she kept it up, she would be carving wood toys and statues just like her grandpa.

~ ~ ~

When you listen to other people in different generations, you never know what you can learn. When you learn something new, especially from someone you love, you enrich your life in incredible ways. Focus on finding something you can do with your grandma or grandpa, and you'll get to know their new ways.

Grandma Wins A Blue Ribbon!

Every moment you spend with your loved ones can be incredible. Your family can teach you things, and they love you so much. Learning more about them, what they do, and how they have lived life is something you should experience. When you learn more about who they are, you'll grow closer than ever imagined. You may even help them win an award!

~ ~ ~

Smells rose and swirled around Lana as they walked through the fair entrance. Cinnamon, sugar, fries, burgers, and meatball scents greeted her. Besides being at her grandma's farm, the county fair was her favorite place in the world.

She looked around with wide eyes.

To her left were horses with their mane braided with ribbons. To her right were games people could play to win big stuffed animals or live goldfish.

In front of her was the craft barn.

"What do you think?" Grandma said, squeezing Lana's hand. "Do we have a chance?" Lana smiled up at her grandma, whose eyes were sparkling and blue. She nodded.

She really hoped her grandma would win.

A few weeks ago, she was at her grandma's house helping her prepare for just this moment. Some things didn't go as planned.

But, as Lana remembered the day, she couldn't imagine things going any other way.

After her parents dropped her off with her grandma, Lana followed Grandma into the living room. The house smelled like lilacs. It was Grandma's favorite scent, and she always had them in the house when the flowers bloomed. When they weren't, Grandma used lilac oil instead to make the house smell sweet.

But, today, instead of focusing on the smell, Lana walked into the living room and was in awe. The room was covered in large, square, star, and heart-shaped quilts. There were so many designs Lana couldn't take in everything all at once. She turned to her grandma and said, "These are so beautiful! Can I touch them?"

Grandma smiled and said, "Thank you, dear. Yes, you can touch them."

Lana picked up the blanket closest to her. The fabric was soft and cool under her touch. There were small stitches in each shape that created outlines and fun patterns. The stitches were different colors and were bumpy as she traced them with her finger.

"These are incredible! What kind of blankets are they?" Lana had never seen anything like them.

"These are called quilts. And you put them together by taking different scraps of fabric and images. You sew them together and create a unique blanket that will be one of a kind."

"You have so many!"

"Yes," Grandma laughed, "I've been making them for a long time. I'm going to enter a few at the county fair, and the quilting contest is the only contest I haven't won a blue ribbon. At least for the talents, I have. I wouldn't try bull riding or joining a hotdog eating contest." She chuckled at her joke. "I want to enter three, but I need your help picking out which ones to take."

Lana's gaze ran over the quilts. There had to be at least fifteen and she wasn't sure how she would pick three, let alone just one, to be her favorites.

Grandma said, "Just look, feel, and listen to your gut. You tell me the first thing that comes to your mind when seeing each one."

Lana nodded back to her grandmother. She walked up to the first quilt and saw it had a fabric of pink flowers, with white stars stitched into it and a darker pink border. While Lana thought it was pretty, her gut didn't talk to her. Instead, she moved on to another blue and purple one with intricate shapes made out of smaller shapes. "This one is very interesting!" Lana said, "I hope you can show me how to make something like this one day."

Grandma came over and picked up the quilt. "I will make quilting a blanket the next craft we do together."

Lana smiled. She would have something new to look forward to.

After looking through all the quilts, Lana wavered back and forth. They were all beautiful and very different. Each time she would look to her grandma for advice, Grandma would only smile at her and give her an encouraging nod.

Lana bit her lip and pointed to the blue and purple ones. "That one is my favorite." She knew that because she wanted to create one just like it.

"Wonderful. That one will go. Please pick two more."

Lana sighed, "I don't know how to choose."

"You're doing a great job. Keep going."

So, Lana continued to examine the quilts and finally settled on two more. Another was green with a tree shape stitched into it, and the third was simple white fabric with colorful threads stuck through it to make it look like an outline of a garden. Lana thought it was very clever and wanted to do something like it for her quilt.

Because Grandma didn't want to get them dirty, she suggested that they put each into a box. Lana got the boxes, tissue paper, and then folded them up neatly. Each quilt was put into its own box. Just because they were so big that if they tried to add them all together, one box would be too heavy for them to carry!

When they were done boxing everything up, Lana took a box, and Grandma took a box. They walked them out to the car and as Grandma was putting her box into the trunk, Lana heard *Riiiiiip!* Then, she felt the weight of the box drop from the bottom.

"Oh no!" Lana yelled. She looked at the ground underneath her and saw that the blue and purple quilt was now in a mud puddle.

Sadness and tears started to well up inside of her. "I'm so sorry, Grandma! I didn't mean to drop it."

Lana scrambled to pick up the quilt and dropped the box on the ground. She scooped the dirty fabric up into her arms and held it close to her. She rubbed her tears away on the quilt but couldn't stop them from coming.

With her head buried in the quilt, Lana felt a gentle touch on her back.

"Lana," she heard.

Lana looked up to see her grandma's kind face looking down.

She sniffled a little.

"It's okay. We can fix it." Grandma's voice was soft and relaxed. "Fabric is easy to wash, and quilts are easy to fix. Okay?"

Lana nodded again. She shifted the quilt into one arm and rubbed away the tears off her cheek with her free hand.

"Let me take it. Come on, let's see what we can do to fix the problem."

Back in the house, Lana and her grandma sat together.

Lana watched her grandma's fingers work quickly to untangle the stitching from the part of the blanket where it was dirty.

Her grandma said as she worked, "Do you know what happened wasn't your fault?"

Lana said, "No." It felt like her fault, and she was the one in charge of the box.

"You can't help that the bottom fell out of the box. We couldn't have known that would happen." Her grandma removed the stained fabric, and she set it aside. "Here, you cut out a piece of fabric, and I'll be right back."

"What do you want me to do?"

"Just follow your gut. Listen to the fabric. It will tell you what shape to make." With that, Lana's grandma left the room, and Lana was left with scissors in one hand and a large sheet of purple fabric in another. She blinked. She had no idea what to do.

Lana ran her fingers over the smooth material. It was thin but felt a little like velvet.

Lana thought about the other shape. It was a heart. But she didn't want to make a heart. But, she could make a few hearts that looked like a flower, couldn't she? She felt the fabric, and that idea seemed right.

Lana started to cut out a heart shape. She figured that they could make eight flower petals if she cut out four shapes. But, while cutting, she went too deep into the blanket and ripped some of the fabric when she was pulling out the scissors.

Lana looked at the heart and saw that it wasn't the same size as the others, and the second shape was lopsided. Lana started to get upset again, and she was ruining her grandmother's quilt all over again.

Just as Lana was ready to burst into tears, her grandma came in the room, "Lana! That shape is wonderful!" Lana blinked back her tears and looked at her grandma.

Lana was confused. "They are all different shapes and sizes. This one has a rip in it."

"Trust me. All of those elements are going to make an amazing addition to the quilt. Just watch."

Lana wanted to trust her grandma more than any-one. So, Lana just nodded. "Will you help me sew the pieces into place? I'll show you how."

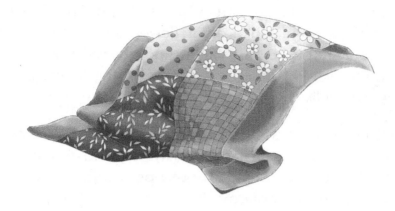

And they worked together for the day, preparing the final quilt for the blue ribbon contest.

The next week, Lana visited her grandma at the county fair. But, she first noticed a big blue ribbon on the blue and purple quilt they worked on together. Joy and pride swelled her heart. She was excited because not only had she picked out the quilt, but she had also helped fix it.

Lana turned around to see her grandma smiling back at her, "See?" her grandma said, "Without your beautiful mistake, I may never have won!" They hugged each other and beamed, "You'll have to help me with all my quilts from now on."

Grandma kissed Lana's cheek, and Lana said, "Yes! I will."

~ ~ ~

Even when you make mistakes, they can turn out to be beautiful. Grandparents are incredible and have amazing things to teach you. If you're lucky, you can help your grandparents accomplish fantastic things. No matter your age, you can always have new goals and reach those goals with hard work and help from your family.

Different House, Different Rules

Do you ever think about what it is like to grow up in different houses? Do you believe that people have different rules than you? When you are with your friend or cousin or aunt and uncle, do you think about the rules, or do you expect them to be the same as the ones you know? The world is full of many people who are different from you and your family. These differences aren't bad. They're just different. When you realize that everyone has a view of the world that is separated from yours, it becomes much larger and can seem even more incredible.

~ ~ ~

"Now," Adia said to her cousin, "Let's see if we need to operate."

Adia held up the blue magnifying glass and looked at her cousin Lily's knee. Nothing was wrong with it, but both girls loved playing pretend doctor. When Adia grew up, she wanted to be a doctor for fixing bones; when Lily grew up, she wanted to be a vet, which is a doctor for animals.

"Hmm, hmmm. Hmmm . . ." Adia muttered. She squinted her eyes and poked at Lily's knee. When she lifted her head, she said, "I think we need to operate. It looks like your kneecap crumbled when walking down candy lane."

Lily tried not to smile too widely and enjoyed her cousin's imagination very much. She put her head down on her bed and said, "Okay, doctor. Operate on me."

Adia put her magnifying glass back into her toy medical bag and pulled out a new instrument. She placed the funnel over Lily's nose and mouth, and Lily closed her eyes. She pretended to go to sleep.

Adia took out her plastic medical tools and pushed them around Lily's knee.

She took another tool and traced a circle around Lily's kneecap. Lily giggled as the tool ran over her skin with a light feathery sensation.

"Shhh… You're supposed to be asleep."

"I know," Lily tried to settle her giggles, "It tickles."

Adia stopped and said, "Should I give you more sleeping medicine?"

Lily shook her giggles away, "No. I'm okay now. I promise."

Adia nodded and said, "Good. I'm almost done here."

Lily laid still for the rest of the "surgery" but couldn't help the smile that blossomed on her face whenever Adia poked at the tickling spots.

After the surgery, Lily and Adia cleaned up, and Lily went to the bathroom. Adia felt hungry and walked into the kitchen. She opened up the refrigerator and saw a bowl of grapes. They were green and looked juicy. She took out a handful and went to close the door.

Adia tossed a grape into her mouth and jumped as Lily said, "What are you doing?"

Adia bit down through the grape. It popped into her mouth and was just as tasty as it looked. She swallowed and said, "I was hungry. I needed a snack."

Lily took the grapes out of Adia's hand and said, "We need to ask my mom first before we get food."

Adia blinked. "Oh," she said. "I didn't know that. We can take snacks whenever we want at our house, as long as they're healthy." Worry crept into Adia's stomach, "Do you think your mom will be mad at me?"

She really liked her Aunt and Uncle. She also liked coming over to Lily's house. She visited almost every weekend because her mom had to go to work on Saturdays. Adia bit her lip nervously, waiting for Lily to answer.

Lily' shrugged her shoulder. "I think it will be okay if we tell her what happened. My mom and dad don't get mad about too many things."

Adia nodded her head. Her cousin's words did not make her feel better. She didn't like breaking the rules. Even if she didn't know them, she wondered what other kinds of rules were different here.

Adia and Lily found Adia's Aunt and Uncle sitting in the living room. Aunt Theresa was reading, and Uncle Tom was watching football. They smiled at the girls when they entered the room. "Hey, girls. All done with surgery for the day?"

Adia showed her Aunt a drawing of Lily's knee and how much better it looked.

Lily' nodded and climbed up onto the couch next to her mom. She said, "Adia ate some grapes without asking." Adia cringed at the way Lily stated it. It sounded like she had done something wrong, and her worry grew from her stomach into her chest. "But she didn't know the rule." Lily said quickly after she saw her cousin's face, "She wasn't trying to break it. She just has a different one at her house."

"I see," Aunt Theresa said. She placed her hand on Lily's head, ran her fingers through her hair, then turned to Adia, "Are you hungry?" Aunt Theresa asked.

"Yes." Adia's voice wavered, "I just had one grape. I'm sorry. I didn't know."

"That's okay," Aunt Theresa said, "We don't usually eat between meals. We want to make sure Lily eats at breakfast, lunch, and dinner" Aunt Theresa smiled, "But it's fine for today. Come on, let's get you a snack."

Adia felt a little better once Aunt Theresa explained the rule and why it was there. She wondered if there was anything else she should know about.

After the girls ate some sliced-up bananas and green grapes, they returned to Lily's room.

"Lily, what other rules do you have? I want to make sure I know them so I don't do anything wrong again."

Lily shook her head and said, "I dunno. What rules are different at your house?"

"I have a bedtime at 7:00 p.m," Lily said.

"Ooh, I go to bed at 8:00 p.m."

"I must brush my teeth before school, after school, and before bed," Lily said.

"Me too!" Adia responded. Not all their rules were different.

"I must pick up my toys right when I'm done playing with them," Lily said.

"Hmmm...we pick ours up at the end of the day." Adia tapped her chin with the tips of her fingers very seriously.

The girls were quiet as they absorbed that information. Adia watched her cousin.

Lily didn't seem too worried, but Adia still couldn't relax. She grew more anxious, wondering what kind of rules she didn't know about; she wondered if she should be taking her shoes off or even sitting on the bed.

Soon, nervous thoughts were circling in her mind, and she had to get up to walk around. She did. And began to pace.

Lily, who was getting a board game ready for them to play, looked up at her cousin, "Adia, are you okay?"

Adia turned around to speak to Lily, and her elbow hit a figurine on Lily's nightstand. The figurine rocked back and forth and then fell to the ground and shattered into a few pieces.

"Oh, no!" Adia said, and she went to her knees to try to pick up the little statue.

"It's okay, Adia." Lily said, "sometimes things break." Lily came up to Adia and placed her hand on her back.

"Hi, girls—I heard something crash. Is everything . . . Oh." Uncle Tom said, "I see. Why don't you two go into the next room and get away from the broken glass? I'll go get the vacuum to clean things up."

Adia stood but couldn't help her tears, "I'm so sorry!" She ran over to her uncle and hugged him, "I didn't mean to. I promise I won't break the rules again."

"Adia, you can't be perfect every time," Uncle Tom said. He knelt to talk with his niece, and Aunt Theresa came up behind him. "We love you very much. Sometimes things break, and sometimes you'll do something different than what you're used to. It's okay. It's all about learning."

"We aren't mad, sweetie. There is no need for you to worry." Aunt Theresa hugged Adia and whispered, "You are a very good girl. We always want you to come over, okay?"

Adia sniffled and nodded. Her Aunt and Uncle's words were just what she needed to hear to soothe her nerves and tears. She rubbed away the tears from her eyes and felt another hand on her shoulder. She turned to see Lily with a big smile, "Wanna do surgery on my elbow? I think I used it too much when swinging with the monkeys in the jungle."

Adia laughed and said, "Yes!"

She gave her Aunt and Uncle one more hug and said, "Thank you. I love you too!" before she followed Lily to do surgery on her elbow.

Thanks to Adia's surgical skills, Lily made a full recovery.

~ ~ ~

Remembering that different houses have different rules is a good lesson to take with you. Not every family is like yours. That doesn't make them better or worse, but it does make them different. Learn how to be respectful and ask about the rules of the house before you do or try anything you might regret.

Family from Far Away

Do you know how big the world is? There are billions of people in it! Do you have family that lives down the street, across the state, or even in a different country? You may discover many new things when you learn where your family comes from. Other people may dress differently or eat different foods. They may speak a foreign language or use different words to describe things. The most amazing thing you can do is learn from them. When you do, you'll be able to keep an open mind and have adventures!

~ ~ ~

Abigail looked down at the plate in front of her.

It was steaming, piled high with green vegetables she'd never seen before, and had mixed meat cubes; it was dripping with some kind of sauce. On the side was rice, but it was yellow, not white.

The smell was new as well. While she couldn't place the scent of the seasoning, it smelled warm and a little spicey. It tingled her nose, and she sneezed.

"Bless you," Abigail's mom said.

Abigail looked up and said, "Thanks. What is this?"

Her mom smiled, "That is a special dinner from where my family lives. We'll meet them in a few days, and they have a different culture than you're used to. I wanted to give you a taste of what my family eats."

"Why now?" Abigail said. The food didn't look bad, but she didn't recognize anything.

"I told you. My family is coming in from out of the country. I want you to try one of my favorite foods my mom used to make for me."

Abigail looked at her dad. He also gave a smile of encouragement. "I can't eat the food your mom makes because of its seasoning. I'm allergic to it, but I've always wanted to taste it. Can you try it for me and tell me what it tastes like?

Abigail looked at the food again and stalled, "You said that your family is a different culture than what we have. What is that?"

"Since they live in a different country, what they wear, how they speak, and what they eat are different than what we do here."

Abigail nodded but wasn't convinced. She tapped her fingers on the table and said, "Okay." She only said it because she didn't know what else to say. But as her mom's words started to sink in, she knew she would have more questions.

She took her fork and stabbed at the food to make sure she got a little bit of all the food. She closed her eyes and shoved the meat and vegetables into her mouth.

Her eyes popped open, "This tastes good!" she said, "What kind of meat is this? Have I had it before?" She got more on her fork and ate it. It was warm and delicious. It tasted a little spicy, but it also tasted like cinnamon, one of her favorite flavors to eat.

Her mom shook her head and said, "No. It's tofu. My family doesn't eat meat. They are vegetarians."

"Oh." Abigail said, "Wait, what does vegetarian mean?"

"A vegetarian is someone who doesn't eat meat."

Abigail nodded. She understood but thought it was a weird thing not to eat pepperoni pizza or hamburgers.

Over the next few weeks, Abigail, her mom, and her dad got the house ready for new guests. Abigail had never seen her mom look so happy. They made lots of different cookies and pastries. They took vegetables from their garden, cooked them down, and froze them so they could cook big meals quickly.

Her mom even brought out some old pictures for Abigail to see. Abigail was so happy to see her mom's family before they came.

"This is my sister," Mom said. "This is my father and mother; these are your cousins."

Some of the pictures Abigail looked at were of when her mom was younger, other pictures were newer, but her cousins still looked like babies.

"How old are my cousins?" Abigail asked her mom.

"They are about your age, but I haven't gotten newer photos from my sister for a while."

Abigail studied the images and started wishing she had some of the outfits that her cousins, mom, and aunt were wearing. "What are these dresses called?"

"Those are *Qipao* or *Cheongsam*"

"I think I would like a pink one."

Her mom smiled at her, "Good idea! We can get you one."

The next day, Abigail waited excitedly in the foyer for her mom, dad, and the rest of her family to come through the door. Her parents had gone to the airport to pick the others up. Abigail was so excited she couldn't sit down. Her grandfather told her, "You look ready to bounce off the walls."

He laughed and kept reading the paper, but Abigail thought it was the right thing to say, "I feel like I'm going to bounce off the walls," she responded, laughing with him.

Abigail tried to occupy herself by watching TV, reading, painting her nails, and finally, finally, finally, her family came through the door.

Abigail heard the door creak open and raced down the stairs to hold it for everyone to come in.

The family shuffled through the house, making all sorts of excited and awestruck noises.

Abigail was suddenly overcome by shyness. The number of people, their bright clothes, their voices, and the way many of them smelled like cinnamon all shocked her senses. She shrank behind the door and watched them hug each other, cry happy tears from being together again, and ooh and aah over the house.

"Abigail," She heard her mom call, "Where are you, sweetie? I want you to meet your grandparents." Her mom started speaking in a different language, which surprised Abigail even more. She realized that it was hard to move her feet. How would she be able to talk to her grandparents if she didn't know how to speak to them?

"Abigail? Come here, please."

Abigail took a deep breath. She willed her feet to move and peeked her head out from behind the door. Her mom came over to hold her hand. She leaned over and smiled. She whispered, "It will be okay. I'm here with you."

Abigail nodded. She felt more secure with her mom holding her hand.

She went out, and her grandpa scooped her up into his arms. "I am so happy to meet you!" He said. He had a gleaming white mustache and thin silver-framed

glasses. His brown eyes twinkled with kindness and love. Abigail threw her arms around him. "I am happy to meet you too," she said.

Abigail took time hugging every person who entered her home. The more people she hugged, the more her shyness melted away. Then, when she saw three kids around the same age as she was, she got nervous again, but this time, she went up to them.

"What do you guys like to play?" She asked.

"We like to play football," the oldest-looking boy cousin said. Abigail's mom had already told her that her family called soccer football.

Abigail blew out a huge sigh of relief, "Let's go play soccer!" She said. They ran outside together. Abigail grabbed her soccer ball.

The three cousins and Abigail played outside until they were called in for dinner. Before they ate, Abigail's grandmother came up to her and said, "I have a gift for you."

Abigail's eyes opened wide. She hadn't expected a gift.

Her grandmother's tanned skin matched Abigail's own. She also wore glasses similar to her grandfather's, and she had big, rosy cheeks. When she smiled, the skin around her eyes and over her cheeks folded in like a paper fan and made little wrinkles over her face.

Her grandmother handed her a rectangular box wrapped in pink paper with a pink bow. Abigail smiled, knowing her mom must have told them about her favorite color.

Abigail swallowed a little as the room got quiet. She could feel everyone watching her as she slid her fingers through the taped paper and ripped the box open. Tears ran down her cheeks when she lifted the lid, "It's beautiful!" She said.

And as she held it up for everyone to see the pink Qipao. It was made of soft, bright silk and embroidered with small flowers under the collar and along the bottom. The dress was just her size and looked like something from the closet of a princess. Her heart swelled in her chest. She couldn't wait to wear her new outfit and feel like she was truly part of her mother's family.

~ ~ ~

When things are new and different, they may feel weird. But that doesn't mean they are bad or strange. That just means you're learning something new. You grow in incredible ways when you learn something new and become an even more wonderful girl.

Epilogue

Now that our stories are over, special girl, do you see how much fun and love your family can bring to your world? When you are feeling bad, or something negative happens, remember that speaking with your family members can help you solve a problem, feel better, and understand things a little more.

Never forget to try new things, even if they feel weird, because you don't want to miss out on something amazing. Remember that imagination and creativity come from playing pretend and will give you an incredible view of the world.

You can bring so much light to your family, and they can shine on you. Do it together, and your life will be filled with love, support, and laughter.

Bonuses

Our Gifts For You

Subscribe to our Newsletter and receive these free materials

Scan Me

www.specialartbooks.com/free-materials/

Stay Connected with Us

Instagram: @specialart_coloring
Facebook Group: Special Art - Kids Entertainment
Website: www.specialartbooks.com

Impressum

For questions, feedback, and suggestions:

support@specialartbooks.com

Nadia Ross, Special Art

Copyright © 2022

www.specialartbooks.com

Images by © Shutterstock

Cover Illustration realized by
Maria Francesca Perifano

Made in the USA
Coppell, TX
03 October 2023